The Great Valentine's Day Balloon Race

ADRIENNE ADAMS

Charles Scribner's Sons   New York

Library of Congress Cataloging in Publication Data
Adams, Adrienne.
The great Valentine's Day balloon race.
SUMMARY: Bonnie and Orson, rabbits, build a hot air
balloon to enter in a St. Valentine's Day balloon race.
[1. Rabbits—Fiction.   2. Hot air balloons—
Fiction.   3. Balloons—Fiction.   4. St. Valentine's
Day—Fiction]   I. Title.
PZ7.A194Gr   [E]   80-19527
ISBN 0-684-16640-2
1 3 5 7 9 11 13 15 17 19   R/D   20 18 16 14 12 10 8 6 4 2

Printed in the United States of America

To Theodora Coble

The Easter egg artists, Mother and Father Abbott and their son, Orson, were coming home from a trip.

Orson looked out of the window and yelled, "What *is* that down there?"

His father and mother looked, too. "That's a balloon," his father said. "I heard there's going to be a big balloon race on Valentine's Day. Maybe they're practicing."

"I want to be in the race, too!" Orson said.

His mother and father looked shocked.

"But-but-but!" Mother Abbott said. "We have a heap of Easter egg orders to fill, and we'd better hop to it."

When they reached home, the Abbotts got busy right away painting Easter eggs. Orson worked as hard as anybody, but he didn't forget about the balloon race.

He spent evenings in the barn, figuring out how to make a balloon.

Bonnie, from next door, came to see what he was doing. She wanted to help, and Orson was glad to let her, because she was very smart.

Nearly every evening they worked.

They knew how to make a balloon fly. As Bonnie said, "You just fill it with something *much* lighter than air, and it *must* go *up*."

"Right," Orson said. "We'll use hot air. It's ever so much lighter than cool air."

They made a big air-tight bag. They hung it upside-down from a hook in the ceiling and heated the air in it with a gas burner.

The bag swelled and pushed against the ceiling.

"Whee!" Orson yelled. "It works. Tomorrow we'll try it outdoors."

They tried to imagine riding it high in the air. Just thinking of that gave them goose pimples.

The next day they hung the balloon from a high tree limb till they got it puffed out with hot air. Mother and Father Abbott and Bonnie held it down while Orson climbed the ladder and untied the knot from the limb.

They moved the balloon away from the tree. Then they tied a big clothes basket to the bottom of the balloon to ride in.

"Do I get to go first?" Father Abbott asked.

"Sure," Orson said. "Climb in."

Father Abbott laughed. "It pays to be dad," he said, climbing in. "Now, hang on while I turn up the heat."

Soon the balloon tried to rise.

"Let go!" Father Abbott shouted.

The balloon started up, but the basket tore loose on one side. Father plopped to the ground.

The balloon crashed into a tree.

Orson was scared stiff. "Are you all right?" he called out.

"Sure," Father Abbott said. "I'm fine. You can't hurt an old rabbit like me. I bounce!"

"Dad," Orson said, "I think we did it wrong. The balloon's got to be much bigger to lift so much weight, and the basket has to hang from ropes that wrap around the balloon from the *top*, not tied to the bottom, so it can't tear loose like that."

"You're right," Father Abbott said. "Let's get busy. Valentine's Day will soon be here."

The whole family worked on the balloon, and Bonnie, too.

When it was finished, Orson gave Father and Mother Abbott a big hug. "Thanks," he said. "You two are really something."

Spreading the balloon out on the ground, they puffed it up with a big electric fan. Orson and Bonnie walked around inside it, looking for holes or anything wrong at all.

They started warming up the wind they were blowing in. The balloon slowly stood up straight as they made the air hotter and hotter inside it. What a thrill to watch!

Now it was Orson and Bonnie's turn for testing.

Bonnie's heart was galloping. She tried to imagine flying the balloon. It was like a dream.

The balloon looked so *big*, above them against the sky.

Orson named it *Bonnie's Valentine*.

They flew it with no trouble at all. Day after day they tested it in every way they could think of, in all kinds of weather except rain or snow.

"What do you think? Can we do the race?" Orson asked. He held his breath, waiting for the answer.

Father and Mother Abbott looked at each other and grinned.

"I don't see why not," they said together.

"Yay!" Orson and Bonnie yelled.

So it seemed that everything was ready. But the balloon did need color and design to be beautiful, so they decorated it with red hearts and blue flowers.

On the morning of February 14th, they packed *Bonnie's Valentine* and two lunch baskets into the trailer and headed for the race.

The place for the start of the race was chosen because the wind was blowing from there toward the target, a big red heart painted on an open field miles away. The winning balloon would be the first one to drop a beanbag on the heart.

"We can do it!" Bonnie whispered, wishing she could really be sure.

At the right time, all of the balloons were filled with hot air, and they stood up together.

Bonnie and Orson were in their basket, excited and ready.

Then BANG went the signal, and UP into the sky rose all of the balloons.

Orson and Bonnie waved. "Good-bye!"
Father and Mother Abbott blew kisses.
"Good luck."
What a gorgeous sight!

The wind was just right, gentle but steady, and the balloons floated along together. The sun warmed them almost enough to keep them up. Only once in a while would a gas burner roar for a minute. The rest of the time, the quiet up there was almost scary. The balloonists could hear each other talking.

Orson was near to jumping up and down with impatience. The balloons went with the wind, all at the same speed.

"Grr-grr-grr!" Orson growled. "How can you get there *first* if you can't go *faster*?" And from a nearby balloon came the answer, with a loud laugh: "You just climb out and float behind your balloon and *blow hard*!"

Orson had to laugh, too.

"Here," Bonnie said, grinning. "Have a sandwich."

After a good long ride across the sky, they could see the red heart on the ground, far away.

But the balloons were not floating toward it! The wind had changed!

"Uh-oh!" Orson moaned.

"Well," Bonnie said, "things are getting interesting!"

Suddenly she put her lips close to Orson's ear and whispered, "Sssh! Watch that little cloud up there—the only cloud in the sky."

Orson looked. The tiny cloud was moving toward the target!

"Of course!" Orson whispered. "Winds blow in different directions at different levels!"

They turned on their gas burner and kept heating the air in *Bonnie's Valentine* till it rose above the other balloons. None of the other pilots noticed right away.

In a very short time, *Bonnie's Valentine* was up beside the cloud—and moving toward the target!

Now the other pilots began to catch on to what was happening. They all started pouring on the heat and moving higher.

But they were too late. Orson and Bonnie waved a happy good-bye to them, and *Bonnie's Valentine* sailed on, right over the big red heart.

While Orson brought *Bonnie's Valentine* down fast, Bonnie dropped the beanbag plop in the middle of the heart below.

Orson landed the balloon in the open field beyond the target.

"Whoopee!" he yelled, while Bonnie jumped for joy. "We did it!"

The crowd ran to meet them. Father and Mother Abbott were there, panting and proud. They hugged Orson and Bonnie.

Then everyone went back to the target for the ceremony.

The judge held a beautiful white box. He opened the lid and showed what was inside.

It was a golden heart on a golden chain!

Everyone cheered as Orson lifted the gorgeous prize out of the box and turned to Bonnie.

"This is really for you," he said. "Without your brains, we'd never have won."

Bonnie smiled.

"Thank you, Orson," she said, "and Happy Valentine's Day."